August Vatter, John E. Spencer

Out of the Shadow

A Drama in Three Acts

August Vatter, John E. Spencer

Out of the Shadow
A Drama in Three Acts

ISBN/EAN: 9783337343132

Printed in Europe, USA, Canada, Australia, Japan

Cover: Foto ©Andreas Hilbeck / pixelio.de

More available books at **www.hansebooks.com**

OUT OF THE SHADOW

A Drama in Three Acts

BY

AUGUST VATTER AND JOHN E. SPENCER

SOMEWHAT ALTERED FROM THE ORIGINAL VERSION AS
PLAYED AT THE VEREINS HALLE OF THE BOYLSTON
SCHULVEREIN, DANFORTH STREET, BOSTON,
MAY 27, 1889, UNDER THE TITLE OF

"A NOBLE SACRIFICE."

BOSTON

1890

SYNOPSIS.

ACT I.

MORNING. — Isabel's birthday. A husband's love and a husband's secret. "Can such joy endure?" The shadow of the past clouds the light of the present. Army and Navy. A lesson in love. "A flank movement and a 'naval engagement.'" The army routed. Waldemar's confession. "*The man you would call father is an outcast.*" The edge of the shadow. "I will stand by her side and defy the world." Questioning the fates. The foreign workman. The courage of innocence. "Here was my name; he will remember it." THE SHADOW FALLS.

ACT II.

AFTERNOON. — Taking counsel. "Do your best, the happiness of us all depends upon you." Proposing under difficulties. Edith's dream. Father and daughter. "It is true; he is faithful." The shadow comes again. The Rat King. Isabel's scorn. "*Of whom are you speaking? Your husband!*" A little light in the darkness. "It is too late — too late." Isabel learns the truth. A convict's wife. "My idol has turned to clay." Isabel's flight. The Captain takes a tumble. Waldemar's return. The deserted home. "*Alone! alone!*" THE BLACKNESS OF THE SHADOW.

ACT III.

EVENING. — "The cigarette of peace." A looker-on at love. "Great Jupiter! I can't stand it!" The terror of uncertainty. "He will surely come; but when?" The meeting of old enemies. BROUGHT TO BAY. Accusation and recrimination. "Cease your mockery, and tell me what you want." The price of silence. "Will money bring back the dead?" A living tomb. The talisman of love. "Your child lives — but not for you." A father's grief. "Do not ruin her happiness, as you have mine." THE SACRIFICE. "*My little one is dead — to me!*" The shadow lifts. "He is gone, never to return." Husband and wife. A confession. "Why have you not trusted me?" A bond of love. OUT OF THE SHADOW.

OUT OF THE SHADOW.

ACT I.

MORNING.

SCENE. — WALDEMAR'S *grounds. An elegant villa,* L., *steps leading up. Balustrade and steps at* C. *Exits* R. *and* L. *Beyond the balustrade a drop showing factory buildings in perspective.* R. *an arbor containing seats. Foreground potted plants and rustic baskets filled with flowers. Before the arbor a small table covered with papers, writing materials, etc.* MYRON *is seated in a large armchair,* L. *Enter* WALDEMAR *and* ISABEL, *as curtain rises, from house. At rise of curtain, lively music, eight bars; four at one bell, four as curtain rises.*

WALDEMAR. Your birthday party. my dear, opens under the most favorable circumstances. All those who love ·you best once more gather here to celebrate the day. I regret having to leave you even for an instant, but I am obliged to go·to the factory for a while. Nothing but duty would call me away from your side to-day. The brightest and best of the whole year, — the day on which the cause of all my happiness was born. (*Kisses her and exit* R. 2 E.)

ISABEL (*looks after him, then comes down*). He is still my lover, though we are married more than ten years. Oh, can such joy, such devotion endure through life!

MYRON (*sits on armchair*). Why not? Your happiness is well founded.

ISA. (*kneels beside him*). Happiness! That is too mild a term. Our language is too poor to give expression to my joy.

MYR. Then do not try to express it. Love your husband as he deserves, and enjoy your happiness while it lasts! (*Slow music. Strings with mute.*)

Isa. While it lasts! That is it. Father, have you noticed lately how strange he is, as if some hidden sorrow was
preying upon his mind?

Myr. No, my dear. What fancies you have! Depend
upon it, Frederick has no sorrow to conceal from us.
He is too open-hearted to deceive any one. No! Cast
such thoughts away at once.

Isa. But, father, sometimes in the midst of the brightest
scenes, when there is no cause for anxiety, I have suddenly
turned to speak to him, and seen his eyes fastened upon me
with, oh, such a look of anguish, I've stood transfixed with
amazement, and then —

Myr. (*deeply interested*). Well, — what then?

Isa. Then he would recover himself, pass his hand over
his forehead and smile as if nothing troubled him.

Myr. Perhaps it was some indisposition. He works
hard. Think how he has built up our factory, enlarged our
trade, increased our fortune. He has much to think of,
much to try him. But a hidden sorrow, concealed thoughts
and purposes, — never! He is incapable of it.

Isa. Perhaps in the past, — in the years before we knew
him, something —

Myr. But we know his past. His life is spread before
us like the waters of a crystal lake, without a ripple to mar
its purity. Think how manfully he struggled to redeem my
broken credit. He would not listen to one word in favor of
compromise. "Pay the penalty of your errors," he said.
"Stand acquitted before the bar of justice even though it
takes all you have." Such a man can have nothing to conceal from either of us.

Isa. But in his native land —

Myr. He has told us of his life there, of his success in
early manhood, that his father and mother died, that he lost
his situation, came to America, learned our language and at
last by mere chance found his way to this place, while looking for work. (*Rises and lifts up* Isabel.) Your thoughts,
my dear, are unworthy of you, and unjust to him. Banish
them.

Isa. (*escorting him to the house*). He will never lack a
champion while you live, father.

Myr. I have unbounded faith in him.

Isa. And I, boundless faith and love. I promise you to
indulge in no more fancies.

(Exeunt into house; stop music.)

CAPT. A. (*outside*). You sailors tell big stories. (*Enter with* LIEUT. MANLY, L. U. E) Pretty women in China! There are no women in the world so — so — I might say — lovely as our American women. Beautiful women in China! Nonsense! Tell that to the marines!

MANLY. As I am a marine officer you fulfil the command. But, Kendrick, if you had travelled beyond the bounds of your own land, you would know that beauty is not limited to any country. Go abroad some time and you will see for yourself that there are beautiful women even in China.

CAPT. A. Go abroad? Then I must remain in ignorance, or leave the army. A convict has a better chance than I, he can sometimes get a — what is it?

MAN. A pardon?

CAPT. A. Oh, no! Ticket —

MAN. Ticket of leave?

CAPT. A. That's it. Ticket of leave. But I must stay — stay where the government puts me. Now if my wishes had been, what is it — consulted — I would have liked to have entered the navy, but my father was opposed to it and sent me to West Point. I went through, that is, graduated and now am one of a — a — noble or valiant band of twenty thousand under orders to — to defend three thousand times two thousand, thirty times twenty and eight ciphers.

MAN. What are you figuring?

CAPT. A. Square miles. Three times two and eight ciphers, three ciphers, — six hundred million square miles, and the army, twenty thousand men, the greater part officers. Take off four ciphers, leaves four, and two in six three times, three and four ciphers, thirty thousand square miles for me to protect. Is that correct?

MAN. It must be. Figures cannot lie.

CAPT. A. It is so. But we don't try to defend the whole. Most of my time in the service has been spent (*takes off cap and walks away from* ARTHUR, *showing bald place on the back of his head*) in chasing Indians and trying to save my scalp.

MAN. (*smiling*). The danger has lessened of late years, Kendrick.

CAPT. A. (*looks at him, then places his hand on top of his head*). Oh! Well, the Indians are not always — what is it — particular.

MAN. We must go on with our preparations for this evening. Also arrange about giving Isabel her presents, and we must make a speech on the occasion. (*Sits* R.)

CAPT. A. Speech! Who?

MAN. No one more suitable than you. As her brother —

CAPT. A. (*sinks comically into a chair*). Me! I couldn't say a word. It's hard enough to talk to one at a time ; but to a number of people — excuse *me !* No, you do the talking, and I'll do the work. Fix everything for the lanterns, fireworks, and so forth. Each one can give his own present, that will save talk.

MAN. Yes. We can manage it. Frederick will not want to be disturbed. To-day has a double meaning to him. His wife's birthday is also their wedding day. Everything must be managed to make it a success. Kendrick, is it not remarkable how devoted they are to one another? They are married lovers.

CAPT. A. That's it,—married lovers,—good— I wish I was.

MAN. You? I always thought you feared the chains of matrimony.

CAPT. A. That's it. A man who can't talk — well is — mis— is — well, people don't know him. I proposed to a nice young lady fifteen years ago, — I lost her.

MAN. Lost her? By the hand of Providence?

CAPT. A. Oh! The deuce! Hand of Providence! Hand of Ned Sherman! He married her, took her to Northfield. They are living there yet, have four children.

MAN. Well, that is not so bad. You are in your prime; Time enough yet.

CAPT. A. Thank you. (*Confidentially.*) Now suppose I was in love, how would — what would be a good way to propose?

MAN. That depends upon the age of the lady, and the different circumstances, the time, place, season, her manner of bringing up, education —

CAPT. A. Gracious! There's a lot to think of.

MAN. It is a delicate and trying situation.

CAPT. A. I know it.

MAN. You might say to her, calling her by her name — Prudence or Patience, or whatever it might be, — "I love you."

CAPT. A. No! I couldn't do that. I must skirmish around a little. Sort of flank movement.

MAN. Then you might take walks, rides, and visit her at her home, and sometime when she seemed to enjoy your society greatly and was in her happiest mood, ask her if she would enjoy this companionship forever, — if she would like to have you ever near, to love. cherish, and protect her.

CAPT. A. That's good. I'll try it.

MAN. You ought to tell me her name.

CAPT. A. Well, — at some other time.

MAN. (*rising*). Then let us go on with our preparations for this evening.

CAPT. A. (*rises*). That wouldn't be underhanded, this closing in on the enemy? Would it?

MAN. All is fair in love and war.

CAPT. A. (*looks off* R.). That's it! Here comes Frederick.

MAN. Now we can ask him if he has any further orders for this evening.

(*Enter* WALDEMAR *and* JAMES, R. U. E.)

WALDEMAR (*a roll of paper in his hand. Bows to* CAPT. *and* LIEUT.). Wait a moment, I have a few business affairs to arrange. (*They bow and go up stage.*) Tell Whitcomb to give the help a half holiday.

JAMES (L. C.). With full pay, sir?

WAL. (*sits at small table*, R.). Assuredly. It would be no holiday to them if they lost their wages. I will look over these accounts, you can return for them later. Let all further business affairs remain until to-morrow. To-day I would like to forget the factory and its cares. Is there anything else of importance?

JAMES. Yes, sir. The foreman in the spinning-room says, the spinners are using up the last of the cotton, and can't have the new supply for three weeks. Mr. Whitcomb says they must run on short time or shut down at the end of the week.

WAL. (*thoughtfully*). We must try to avoid this error in future and keep an abundance of stock on hand. I will tell the manager not to shut down but give employment to the married men, and others who may have children or parents to support. The loss should fall on those who can bear it without suffering.

JAMES. Linfield asked me to tell you that there is a new workman in the weaving room who is causing them trouble; he would like to have you see about him to-morrow.

WAL. I will do so. I have told Linfield not to discharge one of the help without my knowledge. I do not want any harshness or injustice.

JAMES. That is why he has waited, knowing that you wish to judge yourself in such matters. But this fellow is of a bad sort, and is having an evil influence over some of the rougher kind in the factory. He is a foreigner and harangues to them on their rights. Your wife's uncle recommended him.

WAL. A communist most likely.

JAMES. I think so, he looks as though he had a bad record.

WAL. If he is inclined to do right now, his past should not stand in his way, but I will see to it in the morning. Tell the manager not to disturb me to-day if he can help it.

JAMES. Very well, sir. (*Exit* R. U. E.)

CAPT. A. (*comes down*). Have you any commands for me?

WAL. Have everything properly managed for this evening. Let there be music and a dance for our people on the lawn. I would like to see them happy.

CAPT. A. I will see to everything. (*Exit* R. U. E.)

MAN. (*coming down*). Frederick, I need your advice and help. I wished to tell you, Frederick, —

WAL. Well! Go on. I'm listening.

MAN. You are busy perhaps. I will wait until you are at leisure.

WAL. (*leans back*). Confide your trouble to me. Am I not ever your friend?

MAN. (*sits at* L. *of table*). Yes, and that gives me courage to speak. I am in love.

WAL. I suspected as much.

MAN. Is it so evident?

WAL. To me the signs are plain enough. Mythology teaches that Cupid is blind, but no one claims that love is invisible. Your abstracted manner, gloomy face, and frequent sighs can have but one meaning. But who is the favored one? Can you not confide in me?

MAN. Yes, but first let me tell you why I love. Fate directed you to this place, and made you an instrument of good to others. You found here a man already past his prime, struggling against heavy odds to redeem his credit and save his family from social degradation. By your untiring energy, clear insight, and noble devotion — (WAL. *raises his hand.*) Hear me to the end. You saved him and his family. You were rewarded by the love of those you labored for, Myron Arnold's gratitude, his lasting friendship, the respect of his family and friends, and, best of all, Isabel crowned your happiness with her own noble heart. (WAL. *turns away.*) Out of all this grew up the paradise of your home. Your home has been the nursery of my heart. I have counted the hours when homeward bound that brought me nearer to you and that happy fireside, where I have learned what it is to love and be loved.

WAL. And welcome you have ever been, Arthur; our home circle is broken when you are absent.

MAN. (*takes* WALDEMAR'S *hand in both of his*). You give me courage. When you came here among us, you brought a little child. Time has passed and to-day she is a lovely woman; the influence of your home has developed a grace of mind more enduring than physical beauty. (WAL. *turns away.*) I thank you for her presence among us, and ask you—

WAL. (*abruptly*). Spare me! Spare yourself, Arthur! I know what you would ask; but believe me, it is not best. Do not force me to give the reason, but accept my decision, in the name of our friendship.

MAN. You cannot realize the pain you cause me.

WAL. (*harsh tone*). Devote yourself to your profession and forget her!

MAN. Forget? Can we control memory? Leave her? Why? Frederick, this is no boyish fancy. I loved her as a child, when scarcely more than a boy myself, I love her now with all the strength of manhood.

WAL. (*rises*). I'm very sorry for you.

MAN. (*grasps his arm*). I implore you to tell me your reason. In the name of justice, in the name of our friendship, speak, Frederick! I'm no coward!

WAL. (*looks at him sadly*). You will have it so, but, remember, I would have spared you. (*Sits.*) When I brought Edith here I told Isabel and her father, that she was an orphan, and I told the truth. Her mother was dead. I had seen the earth close over her coffin, and when the last rites had been performed, I took the child in my arms, and returned to my native city. I cared for her as if she was my own, cared for her as a man should who had pledged his honor to — her father.

MAN. Her father?

WAL. Yes! I heard of the destitute condition of his family and promised him I would aid his wife and child. I arrived too late to save the mother, but I have kept my promise and done all I could for his daughter.

MAN. You have, indeed, nobly kept your pledge. But her father? Why could he not care for them?

WAL. (*reluctantly ; turning away*). He was — in prison.

MAN. (*grasping the chair*). Where?

WAL. (*firm, hard tone*). In prison.

MAN. What for?

WAL. (*aside*). Oh, this is torture! (*Aloud.*) For highway robbery. Yes, the man you would call father was an outcast, the companion of thieves and murderers, a man who made a business of crime, a man —

MAN. Horrible! (*Sinking into a chair.*)

WAL. The man lives. His name is Ramenoff, Johann Ramenoff. He was under sentence for twenty years — he has served sixteen — in four years he will be free. What then?

MAN. (*looking up*). Frightful!

WAL. Can you, dare you, take such a risk?

MAN. (*rises slowly, leans on chair*). I can, and I will.

WAL. Remember, Arthur, I have done my duty as a friend.

MAN. Her father's crimes shall not be the means of injury to her. From her own lips I will learn my fate, and if she loves me, I will stand by her side, and defy the world.

(*Exit* MANLY *into house.*)

WAL. (*after a pause*). And learn what it is to have one's life haunted by a ghastly phantom, which naught but death can take away. (*Sinks into chair at* R.)

(*Enter* CAPTAIN ARNOLD, R. U. E., *with a box containing pistols ; places them at small table,* L.)

CAPT. A. We will have target shooting this afternoon, A prize for the best shot. (*Looks at* WAL.) You are ill! What's the matter? Shall I bring you a glass of wine?

WAL. (*wearily*). No. It will soon pass. I have a pain here. (*Places his hand on his temple.*)

CAPT. A. (*puts his hand on* WALDEMAR'S *forehead*). Why! your head throbs as though it would burst.

WAL. (*gently removing his hand*). It is nothing. A slight headache. (*Points at box.*) Pistols?

CAPT. A. Yes.

WAL. Are they loaded?

CAPT. A. Yes. But I will lock the box. (*Feels in his pocket.*) I forgot the key.

WAL. You had better take them away; some one might be injured.

CAPT. A. I will find the key and return soon. (*Turns to go; comes back.*) Frederick, I want to confide in you. I'm in love.

WAL. Another one! This seems to be lover's day.

CAPT. A. Another one? Who is the first one?

WAL. I cannot betray family secrets.

CAPT. A. To be sure. Well, — now, — suppose you were in my place, in love and so forth, what would you do?

WAL. I should ask the lady if she loved me in return.

CAPT. A. Yes, — that's it. But — how would you go about it?

WAL. Who is it?

CAPT. A. Well, — I will tell you some other time. I wanted to know some way to get at the subject.

WAL. Is it our neighbor? Miss Eunice?

CAPT. A. Eunice, Eunice Brown? Absurd! — forty at least, and thin as a rifle barrel.

WAL. An estimable lady.

CAPT. A. No doubt. But I'm not a Methuselah. Now, what would you say to a young lady eighteen or twenty?

WAL. I should say there was too great a difference in your ages, but if you love each other, you will learn the language of affection without any advice from me.

CAPT. A. Language of affection! that's good!

WAL. (*slightly amused*). There is a language unspoken and yet most expressive, the language of the eye, —

CAPT. A. (*interrupting*). Look in her eye?

WAL. (*laughs slightly*). Yes!

CAPT. A. That's good. I'll try it.

(*Enter* L. U. E., ISABEL, MAMIE, *and* EDITH; MAMIE *has a bouquet.*)

WAL. Be sure to bring the key to this box.

CAPT. A. I will. Don't mention a word of this to my sister.

WAL. I'll be silent. (*Exit* CAPT. A. *into house.*) Well, my little darling, where did you find the posies?

MAMIE (*runs to him*). In our garden. They are for you, papa.

WAL. (*sits at small table; takes* MAMIE *on his knee*). Thank you, they are beautiful. (*Kisses her and holds bouquet.*)

MAMIE. Papa, you did not always live here ?

ISA. (*comes down*). Hush, child !

WAL. Let her talk, Isabel. She means no harm. Why do you say that, dear ?

MAMIE. Oh, because I thought I would like, when I am a big girl, to go where you lived when you were a little boy.

WAL. (*smooths back her hair*). So you may — perhaps — sometime.

MAMIE. Oh, I'm so glad. And I will see your folks, and where you lived. Have I any little cousins there ?

WAL. (*puts her down and lays bouquet on table*). We will talk about it some o:her time, my dear.

ISA. (*takes* MAMIE *by the hand*). You annoy papa. Sometime I will tell you all about it.

(*Enter* CAPT. A. *from house, with a key in his hand.*)

CAPT. A. (*locking pistol box*). There. No danger now. By the way, I just saw Derblay driving by.

ISABEL. Yes ?

CAPT. A. Good fellow ; but afraid of his wife. She holds the purse. That's always a bad — what is it ? — condition — state — predicament. That's it. Predicament for a man to be in.

ISABEL. He is well punished.

EDITH. And what is his crime ?

CAPT. A. He claimed to be a Count, but he has no right to the title until his uncle dies. He kept this fact out of sight, though, until after the wedding.

EDITH. I think he loves her.

ISA. Love is no excuse for crime.

CAPT. A. Your high notions about honor were always too much for me. If I went wrong, Heaven defend me from your justice.

WAL. I agree with you. Kendrick, the laws of the Medes and Persians, the old law of hard, unflinching reparation, is out of place in a Christian country. Why is it, Isabel, that you, who are so kind to the unhappy, can be so hard toward an evil-doer ?

ISA. Pity is wrongly directed when it offers excuses for

evil. Toward the sorrowing and unhappy our hearts should turn in the spirit of love; toward the guilty and sinful, in stern unbending justice.

WAL. Who has greater cause for sorrow than the criminal? Who more unhappy than he? Even the law has some regard for him. After he has served his term of imprisonment, it says, "Go! try to redeem your past; you have paid the penalty — you are free."

CAPT. A. That's it, I'm on that side.

ISA. I cannot help my aversion to such people. The respectable —

WAL. (*suppressed voice*). The respectable! I despise the word. It is often the excuse for cruelty. These Pharisees and hypocrites, — they pray for the sinner one day in the week, and on six days turn from him or seek to crush him. (*Knocks the bouquet to the floor.*)

ISA. (*taking hold of his arm*). Do not excite yourself. It is a matter of opinion.

WAL. (*calmly*). Forgive me. Let us avoid this subject in the future.

ISA. (*soothingly*). I will never refer to it again. Surely, it does not concern us who are all the world to each other. (CAPT. A. *and* EDITH *go up stage.*)

MAMIE (*picks up flowers and gives them to her father*). Papa, you have thrown away the flowers I gave you.

WAL. (*takes them*). I'm sorry, my darling; I did not mean to.

ISA. (*embracing him*). You'll not be long away.

WAL. Not long! I must go to the factory once more.

ISA. Come, Edith.

(*Exit* ISABEL, EDITH, *and* MAMIE *in house.*)

CAPT. A. Isabel has high notions.

WAL. Her father is to blame for this. What we learn in childhood clings to us through our whole life. I'm sorry to leave you, but I must return these accounts.

CAPT. A. (*going up stage with him*). I would like a few more points on that subject. We were interrupted and so forth. You think the eye expresses the feeling of the heart?

WAL. Yes!

CAPT. A. Hm! That's a good point; I will hold on to that.

(*Exit* WALDEMAR *and* CAPT. A., L. U. E. *Enter* MANLY, L.)

MAN. (*goes to small table*, L.). I tried to speak to her, but my courage failed. How easy it would have been if— (*Takes a rose from bouquet.*) I will consult this flower. (*Plucks petals from rose.*)

> " Does her heart to me incline ?
> Shall I ever call her mine ?
> Emblem of her mind so pure!
> Will that love through time endure ? "

Childish nonsense ! (*Goes toward house.*)

(*Enter* EDITH *from house.*)

EDITH. Why do you stay here, when it is so pleasant in the house ? (MANLY *continues to pluck the petals.*) What are you doing?

MAN. (*with mock dignity*). Her heart inclines. Call her mine. Love endures —

EDITH. Her love endures ? Will you trust to a flower ?

MAN. This is my oracle. Do you believe in the language of flowers ?

EDITH. A little ; do you?

MAN. When my hopes are encouraged. I will try one of the children's rhymes. — One, I love ; two, I love ; three, I love, I say ; four, I love with all my heart ; five, I cast away.

EDITH. Oh, that would be unkind. (*Looks closely at rose.*) How silly it seems.

MAN. To be like children?

EDITH. Yes. when we are old enough to be sensible.

MAN. I would like to have the hope and faith of my boyhood remain with me through life. We were very happy in those days, Edith.

EDITH (*looking down*). Yes, I— Don't you want to know the answer of the flower?

MAN. (*smiling*). I'm afraid there are not enough petals. Six, she loves ; seven, he loves ; eight, they both love ; nine, they court ; ten, they tarry ; eleven, engaged ; eleven — There are no more petals. (*Looks over rose.*)

EDITH (*examines bouquet*). Here is a larger one.

MAN. That will not do. I must abide by the decision of this one. I might control the oracle by consulting the flowers until I found the right one. (*Looks closely.*) Here is a tiny petal in the heart of the rose. Twelve, they marry. (*Looks tenderly at* EDITH.)

EDITH (*looking at the rose and avoiding his glance*). Oh, Arthur, this one is blighted. That's a bad sign.

MAN. It counts one, and the oracle has answered as I wish.

EDITH. Now if we had a daisy blow or a thistle, we could (*blows on the rose*) see if mother wants me.

MAN. You are not serious, but I am.

EDITH. But if the rose had not answered you as you would like ; if it said, she does not love, or loves a little?

MAN. In love there can be no such word as little ; it is all or nothing.

EDITH (*looking down*). It must be enjoyable in clear weather to glide over the sea in a noble ship. I have not been on the ocean since I was a little girl three years old. Even that experience has faded from my memory.

MAN. Do you remember your parents ?

EDITH. I can just faintly recall my mother and how I cried when she was buried.

MAN. Would you like to live at sea, away from land for months, parted from friends ?

EDITH. I would enjoy it, if I was with some one who cared for me. But that would be impossible.

MAN. Suppose you were with a brother or husband?

EDITH. Oh ! That is against the rules unless my hus — brother was a captain.

MAN. (*smiling*). So you have learned one of the rules ?

EDITH (*embarrassed*). I have been told that it was so. (*Hands him a rose.*) Would you like to learn more from the flowers ?

MAN. Not from them, but from you.

EDITH. Shall I become your oracle ?

MAN. No! Be my judge. I will not trust my fate to a flower that might not answer me as I wish.

EDITH (*looking at bouquet*). I would like to. bring some roses and forget-me-nots to mother.

MAN. Hear my appeal and be my judge.

EDITH (*points off*, L.). Will you gather some of those white roses for me ?

MAN. I will, but first —

EDITH. Please !

MAN. I will obey your commands.

(*Exit* MANLY, L. 2 E.)

EDITH (*looking after him*). The white roses, yes, and forget-me-nots, — some pansies, the purple ones, and lilies, yes.

(*Enter* RAMENOFF, R. 1 E.)

EDITH (*turns and sees him*). What do you wish, sir?

RAMENOFF (*hoarse voice*). Pardon me, my pretty lady. I found your gate open. I came in. It was easy that one should enter this place.

EDITH. Whom are you, sir? What do you want?

RAME. I am a workman in the factory. What do I want? I cannot tell it to you.

EDITH. Whom would you like to see?

RAME. Frederick Waldemar.

EDITH. He lives here.

RAME. Then I will sit down.

EDITH. He is away.

RAME. I shall wait for him.

EDITH. He may not return for some time.

RAME. I see, you do not like me to be here. Very well. I shall go. (*Sits at small table and writes.*) I forgot my visiting cards. He shall know that I was here. Here was my name. He will remember that name.

(*Enter* LT. MANLY, *with bouquet*, L. 2 E. ; *looks at them.*)

RAME. You are not afraid of me?

EDITH. Why should I fear you?

RAME. It was the courage of the innocent.

MAN. (*comes down*). Who are you?

RAME. That was my business.

MAN. You ruffian! (*Points* R.) Go.

ED TH (*clings to him*). Arthur, do not quarrel with him.

MAN. Give some excuse for your behavior or I will throw you out.

RAME. I come to see Frederick Waldemar; he was not here, so I shall go away.

MAN. Tell me who you are.

RAME. A workman — I told her so ; there you'll find my name. Now I shall go, but I come again. (*Strikes match to light pipe.*)

EDITH (*stands between them*). He has done no harm.

MAN. Don't light that pipe here. Wait till you are off the grounds. Do you hear? (*Raises his hand.*)

RAME. (*retreating slowly; aside*). Once I would have choked him, the young puppy. Bah! Nonsense! fool!

(*Exit*, R. 1 E.)

MAN. (*holds her tenderly*). Did this fellow frighten you!

EDITH. No.

MAN. You are trembling!

EDITH. Oh, how wretched he looks! You were too harsh with him, Arthur. Think what a life of misery he must have known. (*Leaves him and goes to table* L.) Here is his name, Johann Ramenoff.

MAN. (*springs forward*). What did you say?

EDITH (*points to paper*). Ramenoff.

MAN. (*seizes the paper*). Impossible!

EDITH. What is the matter?

MAN. (*assumed indifference*). Oh, I was surprised. I've heard of this name. I thought it might be — no! (*Aside.*) Impossible!

(*Enter* WALDEMAR, L.U.E.)

EDITH (*goes up stage*). Perhaps you have heard of him somewhere in foreign lands. Oh, how unhappy he looks!

WAL. (*looks at* EDITH, *smiling*). You are disturbed. Is he disagreeable?

EDITH. Oh, no! I've no complaint to make.

WAL. (*smooths back her hair*). I hope you may never have cause for one. May you be happy. (*Exit* EDITH *into house.* WALDEMAR *sees her to the door and goes over to* ARTHUR, *who is* R., *looking at paper.*) Is that document interesting, Arthur?

MAN. Are you sure he is still in prison?

WAL. Who?

MAN. Ramenoff. (*Music till fall of curtain.*)

WAL. Yes.

MAN. You are wrong. He is here. Look. (*Gives paper.*)

(WAL. *takes paper and reads; staggers to table,* R., *rings bell violently.* LT. MANLY *rushes to his assistance. Enter* JAMES.)

WAL. James, if any one calls tell them I am not at home. Do you understand? — not at home.

JAMES. Yes, sir.

(*Enter from house* ISABEL *and* CAPTAIN. ISABEL *comes to* WALDEMAR'S *assistance.* CAPTAIN *up stage.* LT. MANLY *back of* WALDEMAR'S *chair.*)

ISA. Oh, Frederick, you are ill!

WAL. (*rising*). No, no! It is nothing. I have told James to tell every one who calls that I am not at home. I wish to be alone with you, Isabel, for to-day is your birthday.

(*Music slightly crescendo until fall of curtain.*)

CURTAIN.

ACT II.

AFTERNOON.

SCENE. — *A large, richly furnished room. Door* C. ; D. R. *and* L. C. *door leads to garden.* LT. MANLY *and* WALDE-MAR *discovered.* WALDEMAR *walks nervously up and down.*

MAN. (*sits* R. C.).   It seems odd to me that this fellow can have such disturbing influence. You do not seem like yourself.

WAL.   I cannot bear excitement as I could when I was your age.   Time increases our burdens, but unfortunately it does not improve our ability to face them.   To see the result of years of labor swept away in a moment, to have one's reputation, the happiness of those we love, destroyed by revenge, hate, or jealousy, these are but a few of the ills some are obliged to meet.

MAN.   Surely this man has no such power here ?

WAL.   I spoke of this more as an example.

MAN.   Do not trouble yourself on my account.   My course is clear.   Were he more degraded than he is, I would not let him stand between me and Edith.   Can you not induce him to leave ?   Refuse to tell him where his daughter is.   Let us go to him at once ; offer him assistance, provided he agrees to our terms.   Do you know where he can be found ?

WAL.   I have sent James to the overseer to inquire where he lives.

MAN.   Then as soon as he returns I will go and try to make it an object for him to be silent. ·

WAL. (*sits down wearily*).   You can do nothing with him.

MAN.   I will appeal to every motive and exert myself to the utmost to influence him.

WAL.   It would be useless.

MAN.   Is he then an inhuman monster ?   He must have some feeling.

WAL.   He was revengeful when much younger.   Years in prison, with plenty of time to indulge his hatred, have not improved him.   I must see him alone.   I can manage it much better.   The presence of another might prove harmful.

(*Desperately.*) There is no other way — I must see him and alone.

MAN. But what harm can he do? Edith is of age and can choose her companions. He can make known to her who he is, but he cannot claim her. She would pity him, to be sure; but I cannot, I will not believe she would allow him to part us. What injury can he do? What is there to fear?

WAL. Everything. More than I can tell you.

MAN. I confess I do not comprehend.

WAL. I know the man, and what he is capable of. He has a strange nature — good qualities, but they are distorted, and instead of making him better only serve to make him dangerous. There may be some way of influencing him. Heaven help me to find it. (*Enter* JAMES, C. D.) James, have you succeeded?

JAMES. Yes, sir. (*Hands paper to* WALDEMAR.)

WAL. (*reads*). This will do; I can find him. There is nothing further, he has made no more trouble?

JAMES. No, sir.

WAL. Very well. (*Exit* JAMES, D. L. *To* MANLY.) Arthur, if anything should happen that I fail, if this man should injure, even disgrace me, if all should turn away — would you still stand by me, believe in me, trust me? Would you also change?

MAN. (*takes his hand*). No! I do not understand why you fear his influence, or why you dread to meet this man, and I do not even ask you to tell me; but be assured, my love for you is second only to my devotion to Edith, and will never change.

WAL. (*turns away; takes hat and cane*). I will not delay another moment. I will see him at his house and return as soon as possible. (*Shakes hands with* MANLY.)

MAN. Do your best. Remember my happiness depends upon it.

WAL. More than that — the happiness of us all.

(*Exit* C. D.)

MAN. (*lost in thought*). The happiness of us all? How can this fellow control the happiness of those infinitely above him?

(*Enter* CAPTAIN ARNOLD, D. R.)

CAPT. A. This is the worst — hm! — specimen of a birthday festival I have ever seen. Can you tell me where my gloomy brother-in-law is?

MAN. He has gone for a walk.

CAPT. A. I wanted to see him. We had a little conversation on a — subject of interest, great interest, and — (LT. MANLY *pays no attention.*) Are you asleep? Everybody seems to be dreaming. Have you noticed it? I say! There is some kind of a — of a — what is it, epidemic here; even our Edith has a far-away sort of a look.

MAN. Edith?

CAPT. A. I say that Edith doesn't seem so — so — jolly. She's not enjoying the day as one ought. But she is charming. Did you notice how lovely she looked at dinner?

MAN. She appears the same to me always.

CAPT. A. You hardly spoke to her. You were seated by her side, you should have passed the dishes — I was opposite — you were in the clouds — I was wide awake. She might have starved if she depended on you.

MAN. Was I so neglectful?

CAPT. A. You sat there like a — what is it? — I might say dummy! Don't be offended. I asked her what she would have — a little more gravy? Some of the pudding? — " Yes, dear uncle." — Did you notice it? No! Well, she did. Then she would say, "A little butter, please," " I would like some salt." When I passed her the articles she would say, " Thank you, dear uncle." Did you notice that "*dear uncle*"? No! Oh, it's all right, I like it. I suppose she feels as though we are related. But after all I'm afraid we'll lose her.

MAN. How?

CAPT. A. Why — she will probably be married. I tell you, my boy, that charming girl ought to be kept in the family. We must keep her with us.

MAN. You seem to be quite excited over it.

CAPT. A. Well, yes. I'm used to seeing her in our home. 'Twould be lonesome without her. I was talking with Frederick on the subject of proposing. He thought I meant our neighbor Miss Eunice Brown. He quite upset me. Nice lady, but she wouldn't suit me. I wish I had more courage.

MAN. You, a defender of our country, lacking in courage!

CAPT. A. Not in military affairs, but in affairs of the heart. I'd rather face a Gatling gun than a pretty woman's eyes. Arthur, will you do me a favor?

MAN. If it is within my power, yes.

CAPT. A. Propose for me.

MAN. Propose! I — you had better plead your own cause. Who is it?

CAPT. A. Hm! Well, no matter. Perhaps I can induce Frederick to find out how I stand with her. You could do better.

MAN. Perhaps she might refuse you. It might prove another case like Miles Standish and Priscilla — she might ask me why I did not speak for myself.

CAPT. A. I'm not afraid of that, she don't care a straw about you.

MAN. Then she knows me?

CAPT. A. Yes, of course. Will you oblige me, yes or no?
(*Enter* EDITH *slowly*, L., *crocheting.*)

CAPT. A. Here she is. Now forward!

MAN. Why, man, what do you mean?

CAPT. A. Propose! You said you would.

MAN. For you? Never!

CAPT. A. You promised.

MAN. You don't know what you ask. (*Goes* L., CAPTAIN *follows him.* EDITH *comes down* R.)

CAPT. A. Then retreat. I think I can make a dash.

EDITH. Again we meet, dear uncle.

CAPT. A. (*aside to* MANLY). Dear uncle! Do you hear? (*To* EDITH.) Arthur has some affairs to — he's obliged to go away. (*Motions to* MANLY *to go.*) I will remain. (*Aside.*) Why don't you go? (*To* EDITH.) Isabel is with Mamie, Frederick is out of sight — circumstances favor me. (MANLY *goes up stage.*)

EDITH. Favor you in what, dear uncle?

CAPT. A. (*looks* L.). He's gone. (*To* EDITH.) There are moments in a man's life when — (*Looks round and sees* MANLY.) He is still here! (*Aside to* MANLY.) Why don't you go?

EDITH (*aside*). What can be the matter?

CAPT. A. Out of the heart are the issues of life —

MAN. Says the poet —

CAPT. A. (*repeating*). Yes — says the poet —

MAN. Ha, ha, ha! Worse and worse.

CAPT. A. This is an insult. Edith, will you answer a plain question?

EDITH. I will try — dear uncle.

CAPT. A. I have looked at the subject from every point

of view — that is, on every side — To be sure, I'm on the shady side of forty, but my heart is young — true love levels the difference — and so forth —

MAN. That covers the whole ground.

CAPT. A. (*to* MANLY). See here! This is treachery. (*To* EDITH.) This puts me out. (*Aside.*) I would like to know why he's so jolly. In spite of him, I will yet explain what I mean. (*As he passes* MANLY.) Traitor! (*Throws kiss to* EDITH.) Angel!

(*Exit* L.)

EDITH. What does he mean?

MAN. (*comes forward*). He is in love.

EDITH (*pointing to herself*). No?

MAN. Yes.

EDITH. What an idea!

MAN. He is serious in the matter, but fails to express himself. Perhaps I did wrong not to leave him here alone, he would have done better.

EDITH. You are jesting.

MAN. He fears you will leave us some time, and thinks the surest way to keep you is to be your lawful protector. I am of the same opinion, but prefer to be the favored one.

EDITH (*archly*). So you follow his example?

MAN. (*seriously*). I have not learned my lesson from him. I had it by heart long before he thought of keeping you in the family. — What do you think of jealousy?

EDITH (*laughs*). You are not jealous of poor dear old uncle?

MAN. No! Though I might be excused for feeling a slight tinge of the green-eyed monster, since you speak so pityingly of him.

EDITH. I am sorry — sorry that he ever thought of being more than he has always been. My dear, kind, good Uncle Kendrick!

MAN. I shall think I have reason to be jealous.

EDITH. It is a luxury we ought to avoid.

MAN. Easily said! But I plead guilty to weakness in that respect. Let us suppose a case, that of a sailor compelled to absent himself for a long time from the one he loved. He would think of her by day, dream of her by night. He would recall the happy hours they had spent together — and how natural it would be to fear that some one might have won her affection, and she perhaps had learned to forget the absent one.

ED·TH. If she really loved, she *could* not forget.

MAN. It is the hope, the faith in her that gives him courage. Oh, Edith, you cannot realize how a man feels thousands of miles away! How anxiously he looks for news from home. With what delight we hail the day when the anchor is weighed and the ship is homeward bound, how we count the days and hours! At last we reach our native land. How welcome the cry from the lookout, "Land ahoy." When we enter the harbor what sweet music to hear the boom of the cannon as the salute comes floating to us from the fort. As we draw nearer and nearer to the shore, how eagerly I raise the glass and look for the one I love. At last I see her at the right of the crowd. The ship comes nearer. People can now distinguish us. I saw a veil, some one was waving it. I heard a cry —

EDITH. Yes, it was I — the Navarre! I could read the name. I shouted, "Father! mother! He is here! He has come back!" Oh, how glad I was! It seemed so long — three years! I — (*Collects herself.*)

MAN. (*gently takes her hand*). Edith, — you were glad to see me, you had not forgotten me?

EDITH (*withdraws her hand*). It is wrong. You set a trap for me.

MAN. Forgive me, I wanted to know if you loved me. Oh, I will not give you up! no power on earth shall part us!

EDITH. I dare not listen. You must not speak so. Let us be for a while dear companions, as we used to be. Leave me, Arthur, I beseech you to leave me.

MAN. (*presses her hand in both of his own*). Leave you? Yes, if you insist; but not forever. Heaven speed the hour when I shall call you mine. (EDITH *kisses her hand and places it on his cheek, then turns quickly away.* MANLY *raises her hand to his lips, then exit.* EDITH *looks after him; comes down.*)

EDITH. Angel mother, guard and keep me; if I dream let me not be awakened. Dream? No, it is reality. He is faithful and true — and he loves me!

JAMES (*without*). I tell you Mr. Waldemar is not at home.

RAME. (*at* C. D.). I tell you he is here. And I will see him.

JAMES (*stands in front of him*). You must not enter; if you insist I shall be obliged to use force. (*Takes hold of his blouse.*)

RAME. Let go. You might tear my velvet collar. Let go, I say — you ape! (*Throws* JAMES *aside.*)

EDITH (*goes up*). What is the trouble?

JAMES. This man insists on entering the house; my orders are to prevent every one from disturbing the household.

RAME. Ah, that is quite different. First he repeats like a parrot, " Master is not in, my master is not in ;" now, " We are not to be disturbed."

EDITH (*goes* L., *with* JAMES. RAMENOFF *down* R.). I will ask his message ; you need not wait.

JAMES. Very well, Miss Edith, but I think — (EDITH *motions to* JAMES) very well, Miss Edith.

(*Exit* JAMES, D. L.)

RAME. (R.). Is it true that Frederick Waldemar is not in the house?

EDITH. Yes. Why do you doubt the servant?

RAME. It is polite to lie sometimes in good society. Besides, I do not want to believe.

EDITH. Will you believe me when I say he is not at home?

RAME. (*looks at her closely*). Yes, I will believe you.

EDITH. And will you be offended if I ask you to take off your hat?

RAME. (*takes off hat, after a pause steps up close to her*). Are you alone here in this house? I was told there was another woman.

EDITH. My mother.

RAME. So — and who is she?

EDITH. Mrs. Waldemar is my mother.

RAME. Then he is married ; and you —

EDITH. Mrs. Waldemar adopted me.

RAME. Hm! (*Aside.*) Strange! Well, you have been here a — (EDITH *looks uneasy.*) But I disturb you? I will wait outside. (*Goes up.*)

EDITH. You can wait here. If you have come for assistance you will not be refused. No deserving person ever goes away from here without receiving help. Can I help you?

RAME. No! you haven't the power to help ; I do not want money. Do you receive those who are driven here by their misery?

EDITH. Yes.

RAME. You have a kind heart.

EDITH. I only do what I was taught.

RAME. Is it Frederick Waldemar who has taught you to be so kind?

EDITH. What do you mean?

RAME. Nothing. I am tired; I think I will go. He may not come back for some time. I walked a long way from the place where I was last week to this village. I asked for food when I came; I shovelled coal to earn it. I was put in the mill to weave, but my hands are stiff. I do not know the work very well, I grow tired quick; I am getting old.

EDITH (*rolls a chair to him*). Sit down and rest yourself.

RAME. (*hesitates and stares at* EDITH). You are very lovely, my good lady. It seems as though I had seen your face somewhere a long time ago. (*Puts his hand to his forehead.*) But it is impossible.

EDITH. I have always lived here. I know everybody around for miles, but I never saw you before.

RAME. You may have appeared to me in my dreams as the Virgin in the old time appeared to the shepherds. Your pardon, my pretty lady. (*Sits down wearily.*)

EDITH (*aside*). Poor man, how I would like to help him. Are you alone? Have you no friends or family?

RAME. I am alone — an outcast — shunned by all.

EDITH. Not by me. Will you not tell me your trouble? Perhaps I can help you.

RAME. My very good little lady, you are kind, I thank you; but you cannot take away my sorrow nor lift my burden.

EDITH. We bear our sorrows easier when shared with others. I suffer (RAMENOFF *looks up*) when I see others suffer. I shed tears with them and console them. Some at first refuse me, but I beg and plead, and at last they tell me. I try to comfort them. When I leave they bid me come again, for they all love me.

RAME. (*looks spellbound at her*). They do right, my pretty one. They should love you.

EDITH. And will you confide in me your trouble and sorrow?

RAME. (*rising*). I cannot — I dare not. — You do not know what I am.

EDITH. Yes, I know.

RAME. (*anxiously*).   What?

EDITH.   An unhappy man.

RAME.   Oh, when did any one speak like this to me!   But it is too late — too late.

EDITH.   It is never too late.   God who rules over all —

RAME.   God!   No, the devil!

EDITH.   No, God!

(RAMENOFF *bows his head, overcome by the truth of her words.   Enter* ISABEL, C. D., *dressed as if returning from a walk.*)

ISA.   The servant tells me you insist on seeing my husband.   We do not like to be disturbed by the factory people.   Mr. Waldemar will see you at the office to-morrow, or you can tell me and I will deliver your message to him.   What do you wish?

RAME. (*looks dreamily at* EDITH).   Nothing.

ISA.   Then why do you intrude?   A respectable person would not force his way —

RAME. (*angrily*).   Respectable!   So I am not nice enough to be here.   But I think I have a right to come.   What harm if I pushed the fellow a little?

ISA.   You have no right to come where you are not wanted.   Go!

EDITH.   Mother, he is poor and unhappy.

RAME.   Do not trouble yourself, my good lady.   I do not wish to make harm.   But you. madam, are hard and not like her.   I am not so fine as the gentlemen who come here.   My shoes are not so shining, and my clothes are poor.   I should be in broadcloth and white shirt. have a tall hat and a cane with a silver head.   Ladies are fond of nice-looking clothes.   They sometimes excuse bad morals, but a bad coat and bad manners, never!

ISA.   You are insolent and undeserving.   You can expect nothing here.   Go!

EDITH.   Mother, I beseech you —

RAME.   You show me the door?   You turn me out?   Maybe I had better stay and tell you a little romance.   Perhaps it will interest you.   (ISABEL *holds her hand above the bell on table.*)   You are concerned in this romance.   Are you not curious?

ISA. (*steps towards him*).   Tell your story quickly and begone.

RAME. It is my duty to tell you. But to you alone. This young lady must not hear it.

ISA. Edith, you may leave me.

EDITH. I dare not. he is so strange.

ISA. Have no fear, child; should I need you, I will ring the bell.

(*Exit* EDITH *slowly* D. L.)

ISA. (*to* RAMENOFF). I am waiting.

RAME. (*follows* EDITH *and seems to have forgotten* ISA-BEL). I cannot tell it. I had better go. When I first saw the light of day I looked on misery, and it has been my comrade all through my life. I am no lucky dog. I bring misfortune. I would not hurt any one now. The pretty little one has made my heart soft. I cannot tell you now. (*Goes up.*)

ISA. You said your romance concerned me. Who beside myself are interested?

RAME. I am also concerned, and Frederick Waldemar, my one-time comrade —

ISA. My husband the companion of such as you! (*Turns away and laughs ironically.*)

RAME. Yes! I tell you, yes! My companion.

ISA. Your story is too romantic. (*Laughs*)

RAME. You laugh at me? Oh, madam, I can make you cry.

ISA. (*alarmed; goes to table* L., *holds her hand over the bell*). You are insulting, I will call those who can assist you to leave.

RAME. That is right. Ring the bell. (*She hesitates.*) Ring it, I say! Call them in! All, every one! They shall hear the story of my wrongs! (*She takes her hand from the bell.*) Look, madam. (*Goes to her and bares his left arm to the elbow.*) A white mark! another! See! Five, ten, fifteen scars. I scratched them with a knife, each year one. When the day came round that he left me, and I did not hear from him, I made a mark here on my arm, and then they told me there was a pardon, and I was free. Free! After fifteen years! Oh, madam, it seemed like fifty years, it was so long! And I said, I will make another mark, but not there. (*Points to his arm.*) Here! (*Strikes his breast.*) On him! He was false to me. He took an oath to care for my wife and little one. He let them starve. Listen to me! They starved! I gave him money! And when he left my cell I stood looking after him. I could not see, for the tears blinded me, and the hot tallow from the candle dropped on my hand, but I did not feel it. Oh, I can now hear the sleigh bells ring as he was driven away. Then I waited. I heard from him, but only once. The years came and passed, and I said, when I am free I will find him ; yes, if I dig him from the grave! There should be honor even among the thieves. He stood up so proud like a king, and the rats they were plenty in his cell, so we called him a king: *Der Ratten Koenig* — the rat king. I fear I disturb you with my romance, madam.

ISA. (*choking voice*). You are mad!

RAME. No! Do you not see how quiet I am?

ISA. Of whom are you speaking?

RAME. Your husband!

ISA. Monster! You lie! Where is your proof?

RAME. Here. (*Takes papers and letters from pocket.*) The letter he wrote to me in prison — and here the notice where he was sentenced. Read it, I say! You cannot read the German? See, here is his name. (*Points to the bottom of letter.*) Frederick Waldemar. (ISABEL *utters a faint cry and sinks into chair.*)

RAME. (*puts package in pocket*). I should not have told you only for the laughing — but that hurts. She is silent. She does not laugh now. (*Goes to* D. C.) There is nothing funny in Frederick Waldemar, the Rat King.

(*Exit* C. D.)

ISA. (*slowly reviving*). He has gone! What a terrible blow to my pride! Oh, what would I give to wipe out the stain! (*Rises.*) Could any one have heard him? (*Looks in the doors.*) No, or they would have come to my assistance. He said they were together in — he threatened to — I must warn him — he shall not injure my husband — husband! And I am the wife of a — I must see him to prove it is false. Alas! he cannot, it is the truth. The look of anxiety that he sometimes wears — it was not fancy when I felt so distrustful. This is the answer to my doubts, and he has deceived me all these years. I will seek my father and take my child. Together we will go far from here. I cannot look upon his face again. My idol has turned to clay.

(*Exit* D. L.)

(*The stage is empty for a few moments, then enter* CAPT. A., D. C. *He carries a large bouquet ; looks around cautiously.*)

CAPT. A. It won't do for me to rehearse on the lawn, I might have an audience. This is a splendid chance — couldn't ask for a better one. (*Stands at* C.) There's the young lady — here is the bouquet. The object in the point is to present bouquet to young lady — make an impression, as it were ; then while she is impressed with my — my kindness, approach the important question, and so forth. (*Holds bouquet awkwardly towards* R.) Will you accept these flowers as a token of my — esteem — and — and (*draws out a paper from his pocket and reads*) may their beauty be a reminder — reminder is bad, I'll fix that — remind you or recall — recall is good (*reads*) — as you gaze upon them, the state of my feelings toward you. I think it would be more to the point if I kneel. (*Kneels ; reads from paper.*) The deepest feelings of the human heart are often hard to express, and that's my case exactly — exactly is bad — I'll fix that. (*Lays down bouquet ; takes pencil and writes.*) Confound the luck ! I would have been all through if he'd kept out of the way. I will make a clean breast of it to Frederick. No doubt he will be surprised ; but I'm in for it, and so here goes ! (*Rises.*) Forward ! march ! (*Goes up stage.*) (*Enter* FREDERICK, C. D.; *does not see* CAPT. A. *Comes down.*)

WAL. I should have waited until he returned, but I had not the patience — no, it was terror. I rushed home, dreading to meet any one lest they should read the secret in my face, startled by the sound of my own footsteps, creeping like a thief through the woods. What have I done to be so tortured ? Shall one misguided act outweigh years of honest labor and moral conduct ? What a coward conscience has made of me ! (*Removes hat and lays it along with cane on table.*)

CAPT. A. (*comes down*). Frederick —

WAL. (*starts*). You surprised me.

CAPT. A. I should say so — you're as fidgety as a woman. Ahem ! I won't disturb you but a moment. I have something on my mind, but now when I come to the point it's just as hard as ever. Hem ! Don't you think it would be too bad if we lost Edith, that is if she was married and went away ?

WAL. I shall miss her, but we ought not to stand in the way of her happiness.

CAPT. A. No doubt. But it might be so arranged that she would remain here. Ahem ! I am willing to have it so.

WAL. They can decide that matter for themselves.

Capt. A.   They?   Who?

Wal.   Arthur and Edith.   I have felt for some time that this would be the result.   Two such natures could not be together long without mutual attraction.   It is for the best, and I shall aid them to realize their hope.   I opposed Arthur at first, but it was useless.   (*Goes to window.*)

Capt. A.   Arthur and Edith?   (*Aside.*)   This is treachery.   (*Takes cane from table, makes thrusts and passes.*) Would that duels were fashionable.

Wal. (*turns and sees him*).   Are you crazy?

Capt. A.   Ahem!   I'm practising the broadsword exercise.   This news surprises me; I must work off my — what is it? — surplus feelings.

Wal.   A singular way you have of doing so.   (*Looks out of window.*)

Capt. A. (*dramatic manner; aside*).   As the poet says,—
  "'Twas ever thus: from childhood's hour,
     I've seen my fondest hopes decay;
   I never loved a tree or flower
       But 'twas sure to" — to — something and so forth.   (*Goes up.*)

Wal.   Are you going?

Capt. A.   Right about face!   March!
                    (*Exit* C. D.)

Wal.   Would that I had so light a heart.   He skims the surface of life, while I am shaken by its deepest trials. (*Sinks into a chair at* L., *buries his face in his hands. After a pause, enter* EDITH, L.)

Edith.   I wonder who he was — he is so strange and so wretched.   Oh, why cannot every one be as happy as I am! (*Sees* Waldemar; *goes to him and smooths his forehead.*) Does your head ache?

Wal. (*looks at her dreamily*).   Have you been here long?

Edith.   A few moments.   (*Sits at his feet.*)   Come back from dreamland and talk to me.

Wal.   I did not hear you come in.   I was thinking.

Edith.   May I know your thoughts?

Wal.   I was thinking of the future, of you and Arthur, — of your mother, of this day so full of interest to us all.

Edith.   The happiest, brightest day I have ever known.

Wal. (*takes her hand*).   Arthur has told you?

Edith.   Yes.

Wal.   Then you will before another year has passed leave us to enter your own home.   This day has brought joy to you and sorrow to others. How mysterious are the ways of life. It seems to be inevitable that there shall be no gain without loss, no pleasure without pain, no success without possible defeat. You are very dear to me, and it will be hard to part from you.

EDITH. Why need we part?

WAL. It is best. The young bird seeks a new nest.

EDITH. But it may be near the old one, within reach of the old home.

WAL. Yes. I trust it may; but, Edith, do not be too sure of your happiness. (*Bends towards her earnestly.*) Suppose anything should come between you and the fulfilment of your hopes, making it impossible to realize them. Suppose you should hear an evil report concerning Arthur's life in the years he has been away. Imagine he had been tempted and fallen, been guilty of a crime, and, though bitterly repenting, yet must bear the mark of this crime deeply printed on his soul through life. Could you still love him and be true?

EDITH. I—do not speak so. If he had fallen it would break my heart. (*Bows her head.*)

WAL. Would you forgive him?

EDITH (*raises her head and clasps her hands*). Yes! I would forgive and cling to him, even though he were guilty. I would follow him even to prison.

WAL. Heaven bless you for those words, but do not fear; your devotion will never be put to such a trial. He has committed no crime. He is all you believe him to be.

EDITH. You were so earnest I feared you meant it.

WAL. (*rising and lifting* EDITH). I wished to test your loyalty. Sing! Dance! Give expression to your joy, for you have reason to be proud of him. Go to him in all trust and confidence, he is worthy of a queen.

EDITH. I would have loved him even if he had done wrong, but I am glad I have nothing to forgive. (*Exit* D. R.)

WAL. She would have clung to her lover if he were in prison, guilty, an outcast, a criminal. A wife ought to be as true. I will appeal to her. (*Rings bell.*) Confess what I should have told her years ago. She will forgive me. (*Enter* JAMES, D. R.) Tell Mrs. Waldemar I would like to see her if she is at liberty.

JAMES. Yes, sir. (*Exit* D. L.)

WAL. It was just such a day as this when I came here, footsore, weary, almost penniless, carrying the little child in my arms. I sat down by the gate to rest. Little Edith cried to see me so miserable. How it comes back to me! Isabel was gathering flowers. She came to the gate and looked down upon us, at first with idle curious glance, and then with interest and compassion. She told me to come into the house, gave the little one flowers, dried her tears. How gently she questioned me. Would I like work? Her father owned the mill ; if I wished, perhaps a place could be found for me — and while she talked caressed the child. She believed me worthy her confidence, and now I must confess, I — deceived her — that my name was dishonored. Where I have been so long the master, I must humbly bow and pray for pardon. Oh, merciful Heaven! give me strength to bear it. (*A moment's silence. Enter* JAMES, L.)

JAMES. Mrs. Waldemar is not in. She has gone to ride.

WAL. Gone? Where is her father?

JAMES. He is with her, and Mamie also.

WAL. Let me know at once when they return. (*With assumed lightness.*) How is it about our evening's enter-tainment? Are all necessary preparations completed?

JAMES. I think so, but I will inquire.

WAL. (*feverish excitement*). See that nothing is for-gotten. We should rejoice! Let the people dance and sing. Let them make noise! They are too cold! You Americans are like ice! Were we in Europe I would show you what it is to celebrate a day like this. It is a great day, James, but how still! one might think it was a day — of mourning and calamity.

JAMES. It is somewhat quiet, sir, but we can easily mend that. I remember when little Bella was born, how they re-joiced. Mr. Arnold rushed into the mill and pulled the bell rope until his strength gave out. Every one came running to the place, thinking there was a fire. I was quite a lad then, and Mr. Arnold set me pulling the rope when he gave out. It was a great day, and he was excusable, for they wanted a little girl and it had come at last.

WAL. (*still excited*). Good! The bell shall ring again to-night. See that it is done.

JAMES. Yes, sir! (*Exit* C. D.)

WAL. How still it is! I feel as if the very walls were closing in upon me. The air is stifling! She has gone and left me here — alone! What if she should not return. — and I should be forever — alone! Alone! (*Sinks into a chair, his head on table. Slow curtain.*)

ACT III.

EVENING.

SCENE. — *The same as in Act I. Illumination of grounds beyond balustrade. Lights down. Moonlight on front stage. Antique table.* L. *Large table,* R. *Pistol box on antique table,* L., *also bouquet* MAMIE *gave to* WALDEMAR *in Act I. Clear stage at rise of curtain.*

CAPT. A. (*entering,* L.). The more I try to liven up the occasion, the worse it goes. It's uphill work. Tried to propose and failed. Tried to liven up the situation with exercise — failed ! My mission seems to be to try, and — fail. (*Goes up and looks off,* L.) That renegade ! Speak of — of somebody, and he is sure to appear. How serious he looks ! If I had his luck I'd sing and dance. Well, he — (*enter,* L., MANLY; *he comes down* C., *looking abstracted*) is a jolly specimen of a bridegroom.

MAN. (*turns round*). Kendrick ?

CAPT. A. (*mock solemnity*). I have spared you for her sake. A less — hm ! — a less — what shall I say ?

MAN. Say nothing — at least, I mean, on that subject ; let bygones be bygones and give me the credit of trying to keep her in the family, for I believe that was your motive.

CAPT. A. Well, it might be worse. (*Takes* MANLY'S *hand.*) Arthur, I wish you joy, 'pon my word I do. Next to winning the prize myself, I would prefer you should be the fortunate one. Let's bury the pipe, I mean the hatchet, and smoke the cigarette of peace. (*Lights a cigarette.*) I would offer you one, but you do not smoke, so I'll smoke for you.

MAN. Do you think anything could make you serious ?

CAPT. A. (*puffs violently*). Yes !

MAN. What ?

CAPT. A. Real trouble. If those I love were in distress or danger I believe I'd come out strong. But I see no occasion for sadness ; then why be sad ? We must set the ball to rolling soon. Lanterns to light, dancing on the lawn, music, and so forth. I propose to have a little surprise, quartette singing. You went back on me, and now we must make up for lost time.

(*Enter* EDITH *from house.*)

MAN. (*turns and sees her*). Edith!

CAPT. A. (*aside to* MANLY). Don't let out too strong.

MAN. (*goes to her*). We have been talking about our arrangements for this evening. (*Takes her hand and comes front*, R. CAPT. *goes up* L.)

EDITH (*looks after* CAPT.). Do not let me interrupt you, dear uncle.

CAPT. A. (*to* EDITH). I was saying that we must hurry with our preparations. I've had to shoulder the whole. Arthur, just a moment. Will you excuse him? My dear! Hm! —

EDITH (*surprised*). Why, yes; if you need his help.

CAPT. A. I won't carry him off.

MAN. (*goes to him*). What is it?

CAPT. A. (*low tone*). Had you just as lief not hold her hand while I'm in sight?

MAN. (*laughs*). Is it disagreeable?

CAPT. A. Rather so. Let me down easy.

MAN. I'll be careful.

CAPT. A. Thanks! (*Puffs on cigarette.*)

MAN. (*returns to* EDITH). Has your mother returned?

EDITH. No! The house seemed so lonesome without her, I could not stay, and father keeps by himself, so I felt quite deserted. Can I help you and uncle in your plans for the entertainment?

MAN. I should be very happy to have your assistance. (*Adjusts her lace shawl.*) Be careful about walking on the lawn, the dew is falling. (*Bends over her.*)

CAPT. A. (*turns away*). Arthur!

MAN. (*low tone*). If you should come to harm, I would never forgive myself.

CAPT. A. Arthur!

EDITH. Uncle is calling you.

MAN. (*to* CAPT.). Well?

CAPT. A. Let up just a little, please!

MAN. I was advising her to be careful, and —

CAPT. A. That's all right. Make it as easy for me as you can. (*Comes front.*)

MAN. (C. *stage*, CAPT. L.. EDITH R.). I think Edith may suggest something, Kendrick, that would add to the evening's enjoyment.

CAPT. A. I am ready for any suggestion. My dear!

Ahem! (*Aside to* ARTHUR.) Arthur! (EDITH *looks down thoughtfully.*)

MAN. Well!

CAPT. A. Do you mind if I call her "my dear"?

MAN. Nonsense! (*To* EDITH.) Does the spirit move?

EDITH. I have it. A rose wreath!

CAPT. A. What for?

EDITH. A rose wreath is the emblem of fidelity. In Austria they hav a large wreath at the wedding, and it is given to the bride after the ceremony is performed. Father would know about it. Oh! it would be splendid. I will manage it. Father and mother together, and Mamie holding the rose wreath, she could repeat a little verse. Dear uncle, you could write a few lines — a little poem?

CAPT. A. Ahem! My talents don't run in that direction. 'Twould take till next birthday party to think of anything. You had better try it, Arthur. (*Goes up.*)

MAN. It is a charming idea. Your loving heart alone could suggest it. (*Bends over her tenderly.*) May the day soon come when I can offer you the rose wreath.

CAPT. A. (*turns and sees them*). Great Jupiter! (*Exit rapidly, whistling,* L. 3 E.)

EDITH. You forget that uncle is here. (*Looks up.*) Oh! (*Laughs.*) He has deserted us.

MAN. I fear I am the cause of it. Well, I can make amends by helping him. (*Turns to go. Enter* WALDEMAR *from house.*) Make the rose wreath, I will turn poet for your sake, and you can arrange the rest.

WAL. (*steps forward*). A rose wreath? For whom?

EDITH. For — I — oh, I thought perhaps it would please you and mother.

WAL. For me? No! No! Not for me! That simple custom is for the young, those who are at the threshold of wedded life. Keep the wreath for yourself. (*Takes their hands and unites them.*) Let imagination, hope, and love bring every charm to aid your happiness, but above all keep nothing from each other. There can be no enduring happiness when faith is lost. (*Goes up stage and looks off.*)

EDITH (*goes towards house, turns on the steps; to* ARTHUR). Arthur, I love you! (*Exit into house,* MANLY *follows her to the steps.* WALDEMAR *comes down.*)

WAL. The die is cast, Arthur, and you cannot turn back.

What a treasure you have won! She will be faithful unto
death. There is no trace of pride or selfishness in her
nature.

MAN. A treasure I shall guard with all my strength while
life endures. I owe this blessing to you. How can I ever
repay you?

WAL. You may have the opportunity to show your courage and devotion ere long.

MAN. You are still in dread of this fellow?

WAL. Yes. Uncertainty is always terrible. He will
surely come. But when? Perhaps when he may cause
deadly injury.

(Enter JAMES, L. 3 E.)

JAMES. That fellow is here again. Shall I let him enter,
sir?

WAL. Yes, I will see him here.

JAMES. Yes, sir.

(Exit L. 3 E.)

WAL. At last! Arthur, go in and see to it that Edith
does not meet him or overhear us. Keep her in ignorance
for her sake and your own.

MAN. (*on steps*). I will obey your commands, but if you
need me call. You shall not be a sacrifice on the altar of
our happiness.

(Exit MANLY *into house.*)

WAL. If he knew the true cause of my fear, would he
speak such words?

(Enter JAMES, *showing in* RAMENOFF. *Points to* WAL.)

JAMES. This is Mr. Waldemar. (*To* WALDEMAR.) Do
you wish me to remain here, sir?

WAL. No! Remain in the garden and allow no one to
disturb me.

(JAMES *bows; looks sharply at* RAMENOFF, *and exit.*)

WAL. (*front* L., *turns and looks for a few moments at*
RAMENOFF; *aside*). Courage! It is he!

RAME. (*comes slowly front, looking at* WAL.). You are
glad to see me? (WAL. *turns away.*) No? I am happy
to see you. (*Looks around and plucks a flower from vase,
paying with it.*) You have a fine place, quite a change it
must be for one who has been under some restraint. Everything is beautiful, fine, and the appearance is changed. No
stripes in the clothes now, my fine comrade. We like the
plain goods better. Heh!

WAL. Stop! Cease your mockery, and tell me what you want.

RAME. Not so fast, my good friend. I have waited so long, I can take a little time now. I have been looking forward to this meeting for many years. I cannot lose one bit of my pleasure.

WAL. Can you find pleasure in torture?

RAME. Torture? It is I who have known that. I had years of it, suffering the torments of the damned while you — you have lived in Paradise. I have some feeling, and I want a better greeting than this after so long a parting. We were in the same boat, my fine fellow; you took a short voyage and I a long one, but we were in the same boat.

WAL. Name the price of your silence, I will give it if it is in my power, but only on one condition — that you leave this place and never return. I have buried the past and atoned for it,

RAME. So! I'm not welcome. You are not proud of me!

WAL. (*contemptuously*). Be done with this. Name your price and go!

RAME. My price? Ah, my good friend, your money cannot buy what I want. There was a time when money could have served, but now it cannot. Will money bring back the dead?

WAL. (*aside*). He thinks they are both dead.

RAME. I was not so bad company for you in the old days. Who was your friend in prison? Me. Whose arm stopped the blow that would have cost you your life? Mine! In return I asked that you should care for my wife and child. I have come to call you to account.

WAL. If you came to me in true repentance! If you were ashamed of the past, but in this way —

RAME. (*excited*). Ashamed! What was it I did? I robbed; yes! A rich man who had himself stolen from others many times the little money I took from him. What of it? This — he stole by the law, I against the law. He rolls on in his carriage, and me they sent to prison. Ashamed? Yes — that I took so little. (WALDEMAR *turns away*.) You turn away from me? I will obey you and stop this idle talking. Listen!

WAL. (*turns quickly*). Hush! Not so loud!

RAME. Hear what I tell you. When you left me sixteen

years ago this winter past, I thought you were my friend. You wrote me, and I answered your letter; it came back to me; on it was written, "Not to be found. There is no such person here." You were gone and you could so easily have left word. You could have written, but no! It was too much trouble, or you thought, "He is buried alive; perhaps he will die and never call me to account." After a time a man from our city was thrown into prison. He was put in your cell. (WALDEMAR *starts.*) That hurts? He! Think of me in a living tomb, what I felt when he told me the mother and child were dead. I would not believe it. I had faith in you and your lying face. Years went by, and at last they told me there was a cutdown for good conduct and I was free. Free at last! I had been very quiet and made no trouble, but in here (*points to his breast*) a fire burns. I left the prison, hid away my little money in the belt, saying to myself, "They must be living. I will save the money for them, they may need it." Fool that I was! I carried my shoes to save them, walked when I was sick and should ride, lived on bread when I needed meat. For what? To find a grave in the paupers' field. (*Breaks down.*)

WAL. (*affected*). Ramenoff!

RAM. (*sudden outburst*). But I threw myself on that grave, and I took an oath, "They shall be revenged."

WAL. On whom?

RAME. On you. For you let them starve as if they were dogs, and stole the money I gave you.

WAL. You wrong me. I kept my promise — cared for them — did all I could to improve their condition. I spent all you gave me, worked at hard, laborious employment such as I would once have scorned, and spent my earnings for them. But I soon lost my place. Some one told my employer who I was and where I had been. He paid me off and said there was no work for me. I tried again — earned a little, was turned away with the remark, "We want no jailbirds here."

RAME. The ruffian! I could kill such a man.

WAL. Then we suffered together — we lacked for food, the mother was sick, when I arrived she failed rapidly — and —

RAME. (*after a moment's silence bows his head*). The mother first, then the little one. *Mein kleines Gretchen;* I can see her now with yellow curls around her forehead!

she could just talk a few words then. Oh, that she had lived! She might have fallen in good hands and been different from me. In my dreams I would see her a young woman good and lovely. I do not call myself a saint, but I'm not so bad either. I loved her — I tell you I loved her. Foolish dreams, foolish! Ha, ha, ha! *Ach, mein Gott!* (*Sinks into a chair and sobs.*)

WAL. (*after a pause*). Ramenoff! They told you wrong — the grave was in the churchyard, not the paupers' field. I placed a stone to mark the spot — placed it with my own hands.

RAME. In the churchyard? Do you speak the truth? They told me wrong?

WAL. Yes. If ever you go back to our country you can find it and see that I tell the truth.

RAME. Back? No, never! But I believe you tell what is true. And the little one — she is by the mother? Her name is there — and the age, like she was the child of — of, you know what I would say? Is it so?

WAL. (*abruptly*). I have told you the truth. Now for my sake go from here peaceably. Go to some distant place. I will help you to do better, give you money, and aid you in starting life over again. You can atone for the past and be honest.

RAME. Honest! You change your tune to me. I'm now the miserable outcast, and you the honest man. But I will not quarrel. You have kept your word to me, and for that I thank you. Do not say to me, go! I shall go when I like and stay when I please.

WAL. (*angry*). Can you not understand there is nothing between us? With your record and your feeling you can only do harm. Your crime was great, mine a trifling affair in comparison.

RAME. Trifling? Your wife, she did not think so.

WAL. (*confused*). What?

RAME. Your wife felt bad when I told her.

WAL. No, you could not, you would not be such a fiend.

RAME. She laughed at me, and would throw me out as if I was some rubbish. Then I —

WAL. (*frantically springs at him*). Oh, you scoundrel!

RAME. (*steps back coolly*). Do you want to go again to prison?

WAL. (*throws up his hands*). You have made the whole

world a prison to me. (*Sinks into a chair near table ; buries his face in his hands.*)

RAME. I did not think — I was mad — but it is not so bad that it cannot be mended. What is it I have done?

WAL. (*slowly rising*). You have robbed me of my wife! You could not spare even her. Your envious nature longed to see her crushed and broken. You looked upon her in all her pride so far above you, and thought to humble that pride, furrow that smooth brow with anguish, blanch those cheeks with fear, wring tears from those bright eyes. Oh, how she must suffer from your brutal hatred! You might have taken from me all the fruit of my years of labor, reduced me to poverty and toil, and I could forgive you. But you have robbed me of my greatest treasure — that I can never forgive. You have finished your work. Now, go!

RAME. I will go. (*Turns to go up.*) I will tell her I lied. I will try and save you.

WAL. You cannot save me. But let me tell you something that may awaken a pang of remorse. You say you loved your child? She lives — (RAMENOFF *attempts to speak.*) Silence! You shall never see her. That shall be your punishment.

RAME. My little Gretchen lives? Not see her? This would be a terrible punishment. You cannot mean it. I did wrong and I'm very sorry for it. I would give a great deal now to make things right. Think of what you do. Tell me where she is.

(*Music from house.*)

WAL. No, go!

RAME. I will go where she is and stand where I can see her, but I will not tell her who I am. Let me see her!

WAL. Never!

RAME. I have wronged you, but still you have a home, a wife, a child, riches and honor. What have I? Poverty and rags. Let me see my little Gretchen.

WAL. (*relenting*). Of what use is it? She is no longer a child, but a woman in whose presence you should fear to go. She is in the midst of loving friends, engaged to be married to a noble man. One word from you could put an end to all this and destroy her happiness forever.

RAME. I promise you I will not betray myself. (*Listens.*) That song! I know it! Who plays?

WAL. Your daughter.

RAME. (*excited*). My daughter! I *will* see her. (*Starts towards house.*)

WAL. (*stops him*). Not there! Here! Look to it — keep your promise. Do not ruin her happiness, as you have mine. (*Calls.*) Edith!

RAME. Edith! No, Gretchen!

WAL. I call her Edith. (*Calls.*) Edith!

(*Music stops.*)

RAME. Even the name I gave her is taken away.

(*Enter* EDITH *from house; she stands on the steps leading to house where the moonlight falls on her. She is dressed in white and wears a lace shawl.*)

EDITH. Father, was it you who called?

RAME. (*aside*). She calls him father. (*Aloud, standing* C., *up stage.*) Yes. (*Aside.*) I did not dream when I thought I had seen that face before. It is my peasant wife before me a lady. (*Goes to her slowly.*) You were very kind to me, and so, as I go from this place now forever, I thought I would like to see you once again and tell you — good-by. (*Bows.*)

EDITH (*extends her hand*). I am sorry you are so unhappy.

RAME. (*about to take her hand, draws back, then lifts the shawl to his face*). My little one!

WAL. (*low tone*). Ramenoff!

RAME. *Mein kleines Gretchen!*

WAL. *Dein versprechen!*

RAME. (*retreating*). Yes, yes! My little Gretchen is dead. (*Going* R. *slowly.*) To me forever she is dead!

(*Exit slowly,* R.)

EDITH (*coming down*). His little girl is dead?

WAL. He lost her many years ago.

EDITH. And he still thinks of her and loves her? Can you help him? Promise me you will.

WAL. I will, if it is in my power.

EDITH (*embraces him*). I thank you.

WAL. I wish to be alone. Forget this scene and be happy, I am poor company to-day.

EDITH (*while going*). Come as soon as you can to see the grounds. Uncle is working hard, and Arthur and I have promised to help him. Will you come?

WAL. Perhaps. Before long.

(*Exit* EDITH, R. 3 E., *throwing a kiss to* WALDEMAR, *who looks after her.*)

WAL. She will be happy. A bright future awaits her. The future! What will it bring to me? Disgrace and ruin. (*Goes slowly to chair at small table; sits.*) Disgrace! Worse than death. Oh, what joy to forget, to sink into oblivion forever! (*Hand falls on pistol-box. Pries it open with pocket knife, takes pistol and slowly raises it. Sees the bouquet* MAMIE *gave him, takes it up; his hand with pistol drops down. Holds bouquet to his lips and then leans his head on his hands. Enter* MANLY *from house; goes to* WALDEMAR.)

MAN. A new misfortune?

WAL. (*raising head*). No. He has gone and promised never to return.

MAN. Thank Heaven!

WAL. Do you still feel the same? Are you willing to abide by the result?

MAN. I am; nothing can change me.

WAL. Edith is waiting for you. Go to her, and make the most of your happiness. "Love's young dream."

MAN. I hope you will overcome this depression. It mars our pleasure. (*Gives him his hand.*) I shall never forget how loyal you have been. I shall always remember with gratitude your untiring devotion.

(*Exit* MANLY *into garden.*)

WAL. I can keep up this farce no longer. I must leave this place before exposure and disgrace thrust me forth. I will take one last look upon all that is so dear. I will bid farewell to the bedside of my child — the dearest spot on earth to me. Here, where I have ruled as an emperor, I shall be known as an outcast, an exile.

(*Exit slowly into house. Empty stage for a few moments, then enter* CAPT. A., R. 3 E.)

CAPT. A. Now for the best piece of strategy I ever did. Eloquence! come to my aid. Mamie must remain with Edith. "Little pitchers have big ears." Father and Isabel shall come here. I will keep on the left flank, and prevent a retreat, and trust to pluck and sharp shooting. (*Goes up to* R. 3 E.) Father! Isabel! (*Goes off and returns with them.*) Head up. sister! Where's your courage?

ISA. (*goes to chair*, R.). My courage is gone. Destroyed by as cruel a blow as ever wife received. You have persuaded me to come thus far, but every moment I feel how impossible it will be to meet him. The very thought makes me tremble. I worshipped him — and now to see him so degraded and fallen, and to think he has deceived me so cruelly! (*Sobs.*)

MYR. (*takes chair*, L.). It was cowardly. I loved him as a son, — trusted him fully. To think that he should creep into our family like a thief in the night. Our family has been honored for generations. There is not a shadow of a suspicion as to our integrity. I am justly proud of our record. Do you think, Kendrick, that I will submit to have it disgraced by a —

ISA. Father! Do not speak the word. (*Bows her head in shame.*)

CAPT. A. (*wipes his forehead; aside*). It's harder than I bargained for. (*To them.*) I don't know what crime he was accused of. I don't want to know, — but I do know that he has been upright and noble ever since he came among us. Let that stand to balance the account. Father, you owe him a debt of gratitude for saving your fortune and your honor.

MYR. He saved my fortune, but not my honor. I will not accept a compromise in such a matter. He gained access to my home, took charge of affairs, and married Isabel under false pretences. Kendrick, suppose you were in my place, and a man should ask for your daughter's hand in marriage. Would you accept him if you knew that he had been in prison?

CAPT. A. I can't imagine it. It strikes me that does not touch the difficulty.

MYR. The marriage was effected through fraud, and according to law is null and void.

CAPT. A. The point is: they are married; we are not to form a bond, but we are trying to — to loose what is already bound.

MYR. I will not make any allowance for such sophistry. No child of mine shall bear a dishonored name.

CAPT. A. But what name will you give to Mamie?

MYR. Mine! A name she can be proud of.

CAPT. A. (*aside*). If I could get farther out of the way. (*To* MYRON.) Isabel is the only one to decide the question. Leave it to her. (*To* ISABEL.) What do you propose?

ISABEL (*reluctantly*). A separation.

CAPT. A. Floored! (*Goes up and returns.*) Two against one. Heavy odds. I can't understand why it is that you should turn accuser and I become his champion. Our positions should be reversed. Where is your love and devotion?

ISA. What I loved in him has gone. His honesty, loyalty, and truth. What remains awakens no feeling of devotion. Look where I may, the walls of a prison stand between us.

CAPT. A. Have you thought of the effect on society in case of a separation? What excuse can you offer to account for your desertion?

ISA. Desertion? He has deceived me for years.

CAPT. A. What can you say to his child, when she wonders at her father's absence? (ISABEL *covers her face with her hands; aside.*) I've found the key to her heart. Father! I beseech you not to be unjust. I acknowledge the appearances are against him. But do not judge him unheard.

MYR. The notice in that paper, and the letter signed by him, are positive proof.

CAPT. A. Who offers this evidence? An ex-convict; a miserable fellow, — perhaps he does it from hatred. Is it fair to condemn on such authority? Come! Give him the benefit of the doubt. Let Isabel see him and decide for herself. (*Goes to his father.*)

MYR. (*rises*). Well, be it so. I fear he cannot clear himself. But whatever she concludes I will agree to. Daughter, remember my teachings. If he be unworthy, do not be persuaded to do wrong.

(*Exit with* CAPTAIN, R. 3 E.)

ISA. How can I meet him? (*Enter* WALDEMAR *slowly from house.*) I dare not cross that threshold again. (*Sees* WALDEMAR *and turns away.*)

WAL. If I am the occasion for your fear, you need not hesitate. I am going away.

ISA. (*faint voice*). You will leave me! Oh, Frederick, you know — that wretched man —

WAL. I know that he met you and told you we were together in —

ISA. Yes. But it is not true? Say it is a slander! I will take your word rather than to believe him. You have always told me the truth. Speak!

WAL. I cannot. I was in prison for two years. (ISABEL *shrinks away from him.*) I was justly accused, tried before a court, pleaded guilty! Was sentenced and served out my term. (ISABEL *sinks into chair.*) In justice to myself and you whom I have deceived, it is best for me to tell the nature of my offence. My father was cashier in a large banking house in Vienna. I was employed in the same establishment and had charge of certain funds and securities. He speculated with the funds of the bank and lost. The time drew near when the examination of the books would be made. My father confided in me, — almost crazy with grief and shame at his crime, and fearing exposure, — he begged me to think of some way of concealing his loss. On the impulse of the moment and actuated by love for him, I promised to try to save him. Unknown to my father I placed in his drawer funds entrusted to me, and all the cash needed to make good his deficiency, — hoping that when they found his books balanced with the amount in hand they would be satisfied. But I was mistaken. They examined my accounts and also those of the other clerks. The chairman of the committee announced that an error had been discovered and it would be necessary to examine the accounts with still greater care. No accusations would be made until they were certain, but they believed they had found the guilty party. Before he could speak further, the report of a pistol rang through the office — and my father lay dying at our feet. We rushed to him — but he was dead. Had he known that I sacrificed myself to save his honor, perhaps he would have stayed his hand. At the trial I pleaded guilty. The judge asked if I could offer any defense, I answered, no! How could I! The law makes no allowance for a son's devotion. How could I prove my innocence? The lips of the only witness who could have spoken in my defence were sealed forever.

ISA. A noble sacrifice, but still a *crime.* Oh, Frederick, why have you kept this from me all these years?

WAL. If I had told it to you and your father when I first arrived, your doors would have been closed to me. Oh, how often has the confession trembled on my lips. Before we were married, I have gone to you determined you should know the truth, but at the sound of your voice my courage failed. I feared I might lose you. After marriage I dared not confess I had deceived you. If you could realize how I

suffered, and still suffer, you would forgive.   Have you ever
had cause to complain of one thoughtless or unkind act ?

ISA.   Oh, no !   (*Aside.*)   My heart cries out to him, but
my pride can see nothing but a prison wall.

WAL.   Isabel, I have nothing further to say — forget and
in future forgive me if you can — farewell !   (*Turns to
go.   Enter* CAPTAIN *with* MAMIE.   MAMIE *carries a large
wreath of white roses; she runs down.* WALDEMAR
throws his arms around her.)   My child !

MAMIE.   Papa!   See!   I am to give mamma this wreath
of white roses.   Mamma, you put your hand this side, and I
here, papa there.   Then I am to say a few words sister
Edith taught me.   Come, mamma !

WAL. (*looks at* ISABEL).   Can you refuse?

ISA. (*slowly takes wreath, stands* R.   WALDEMAR L.,
MAMIE C., *each holding wreath; and* MAMIE, *within the
wreath, holding it up with both hands, repeats verse.*)
MAMIE.

> As your hands with mine unite,
> Upon this wreath of purest white,
>   May love our hearts imbue !
> When a year has passed away,
> Again we'll meet to keep this day,
>   And our true love renew.

WAL.   Shall her simple words be fulfilled ?
        (*Extends right hand to* ISABEL.)

ISA. (*clasps his hand*).   She has taught me to forget and
forgive.   Love has conquered pride.   (*Throws her arms
around* MAMIE.)   My precious one.   You have brought me
back to myself and to the path I shall never leave.   (*Kisses
her.*)

WAL. (*takes her hand*).   Am I indeed forgiven ?

ISA. (*gives both hands*).   Frederick, you have taught me
there is a higher power than the law of man, and in this I
will believe even as I trust in you.   My husband !

WAL. (*embraces her*).   My true wife !

(*Enter all.   Factory bell rings.   Enter workmen.   General
rejoicing.*)

CURTAIN.